Ivy

Book One

Christmas on Dewberry Lane

Cheryl Wright

Ivy

Christmas on Dewberry Lane
Book One

Copyright ©2020 by Cheryl Wright

Cover Artist: Black Widow Books

Dedication

To Margaret Tanner, my very dear friend and fellow author, for her enduring encouragement and friendship.

To Alan, my husband of over forty-six years, who has been a relentless supporter of my writing and dreams for many years.

To Virginia McKevitt, cover artist and friend, who always creates the most amazing covers for my books.

To You, my wonderful readers, who encourage me to continue writing these stories. It is such a joy knowing so many of you enjoy reading my stories as much as I love writing them for you.

Table of Contents

Chapter One

Early November 1880

Dewberry, Montana

Jeremy Hycroft disposed of his foul-tasting whiskey as the young waiter hurried past. His gaze fell to David Carson, an undesirable acquaintance who was trying to force a young woman to her feet. She looked more than a little distressed.

"I say," he said rather breathlessly, having almost run across the ballroom to her defense. "I believe the lady is not interested."

Carson rounded on him; his fist ready to connect with whomever got in his way. Her intake of breath was further evidence she was repulsed by the man standing before her. "Is this *gentleman* bothering you?" He gazed at her, determined to help if she so desired.

"Mind your own damned business," Carson demanded. "What's it to you anyway?"

"Watch your mouth in front of the lady," he snarled, grabbing Carson by the scruff of the neck and ejecting him from the ballroom.

"I apologize on Carson's behalf," he said breathlessly when he returned. "Might I introduce myself?"

She nodded briefly and he continued. "Jeremy Hycroft." He extended his hand, and she lifted her gloved hand to his. "And you might be…"

She smiled demurely, but he noticed her hands shaking. Carson had obviously upset the beautiful creature. "May I have this dance?"

Without a word, she stood and offered her hand, and Jeremy led her onto the dance floor. He pulled her close, placing his free hand at her waist before beginning to guide her around the room.

"You're a good dancer, Miss…"

She raised her eyebrows and smiled. She was being mysterious. He liked that. "Thank you," she said, then stared up into his face. That gave him the perfect opportunity to scrutinize her.

She wasn't very tall; no more than about five-foot-five or six he figured, although probably far shorter without heels. At first, he thought she had gray eyes, but when he spun her around nearer the light, they looked green. Her long blonde hair was fashioned at the back of her head, and her perfume enticed him far more than he wanted it to.

The music stopped and the few couples left on the floor clapped. The orchestra began playing again almost immediately.

"Shall we?" He bowed slightly as he spoke and stared into her eyes. Now they were blue. Was this woman some sort of chameleon? The thought amused him. As they slid around the floor, neither one spoke, although he was sorely tempted to ask about her bizarre eyes.

"Ivy," she suddenly said, and it confused him.

"Ivy?" he said without thinking. "What is that?"

"*That*," she said pointedly, "is my name. Ivy Henderson." She tilted her chin then and stared up at him.

Henderson. Was she related to Mildred Henderson? He'd never met her before, he was certain. He would never forget such a beauty.

"Welcome to Dewberry, Miss Henderson," he said.

"How do you know I'm new here?" She tilted her chin again, and it amused him. Or perhaps not. Was she one of those highfaluting women who looked down their nose at everyone else? He certainly hoped not.

He tried to hide his amusement, but it was too late. "Do you find that amusing, Mr. Hycroft?" She began to pull away from him, but he pulled her closer still and her eyes opened wide. This time, they were gray. How utterly strange.

"How do you do that?" he pleaded. It was more than a little off-putting.

She suddenly stopped dancing and he almost toppled over her. "Do what?" She stared up at him with the most innocent of expressions, and it was almost his undoing.

His hand lifted and he indicated her eyes. "That thing you do with your eyes," he said, waving his hands about. He raised an eyebrow, and to his dismay, she stormed off, leaving him to stand alone in the middle of the dance floor.

He followed her, hooking his arm through hers when he caught up. Which he did quickly since he was far taller than the mysterious Miss Ivy Henderson.

She rounded on him. "I do not do anything," she snarled. "It happens automatically. Most people," she said gruffly, "are not rude enough to accuse me of being a freak show." She pulled her arm from his and thundered off toward the cloak room.

He couldn't pull his eyes away from the pretty little newcomer who set his heart to racing.

"Of course, Mrs. Grayson," Ivy said. "I'll have it packaged and ready by the time you return." She patted the elderly lady on the shoulder and began to fold the garment. She glanced up as she heard low muttering at the door.

Jeremy Hycroft held the door open for the older lady. Such a gentleman. It was a pity he could be quite rude when he put his mind to it.

"Oh, Miss Henderson," he said, heading toward her. "I was looking for the owner. She always looks after me." He glanced about. "She's not here?"

She wanted to turn away, but he was presumably a customer, so she kept her gaze on him. Her voice quivered. "My aunt died last week. You didn't hear?"

He swallowed. "I've been out of town on business. I'm sorry to hear about Mildred. She was a gem." He blinked a few times, and she wondered if her aunt's passing had genuinely upset him. "I apologize that I didn't put two and two together. I should have figured you were related because of your surname."

"My mother and Aunt Mildred married brothers. Uncle Henry died some years ago." All this talk of lost family brought a tear to her eye, and Ivy swiped at her cheeks. Turning her back to the man, she snatched up some tissue paper to wrap Mrs. Grayson's purchase. "What can I do for you, Mr. Hycroft," she said, suddenly becoming frustrated by his presence.

He watched her wrap then reach for a dress box. "It's like watching Mildred," he said then shook himself. "I'm after a gift for my mother. A scarf perhaps?"

"What price range are we looking at, Mr. Hycroft?"

He frowned. "Do call me Jeremy." He smiled then and glanced about the store. "As to price, there is no limit. She is my mother after all."

Somewhat surprised, Ivy placed the lid on the box of the carefully wrapped gown then put it aside. "If you'll follow me, Mr. Hycroft."

He was so close on her heels, Ivy was certain she could feel his breath on her neck. "This is my full range of scarves. Does anything take your fancy?" She watched as he scrunched up his face.

"No, no. This isn't what I want." He turned to her and frowned again. "I think I've used the wrong terminology." He glanced about the store again, his eyes landing not far away. "That's what I want," he said, pointing to a shelf across the store.

"Those are called shawls," she told him firmly. "Quite different to scarves." Ivy knew she was being terse with him, but the man had been quite rude to her at the ball. Was it any wonder she felt bad tempered around him?

She pulled a few of the better-quality shawls off the shelf to show him. "Follow me to the counter and I'll lay them out for you," she said, then turned on her heel and made her way to the counter.

"I rather think Mother would like this one," he called, fingering yet another shawl. Ivy turned back and smiled. It was one Aunt Mildred had made herself.

"That particular shawl is made of the finest wool, as I'm sure your discerning eye can see." She'd meant it as a back-handed insult, but he didn't seem to take it that way. "The woolen flowers would not have been easy to create considering her arthritic hands in the end." She closed her eyes and swallowed. Of all the garments in the store, why did he have to pick that one?

"Did Mildred make this," he asked gently, stepping toward her.

Ivy glanced up at him. Perhaps he wasn't such a buffoon after all. "Yes," she said quietly. "She did a wonderful job, all things considered."

He watched her closely, his eyes never leaving hers. He seemed to study her for an eternity, then he placed the oversized shawl back on the shelf. "I'll find something else." He began to walk away, and she felt terrible. She'd made the poor man feel guilty, and over what? Something her aunt had painfully made for this very purpose – to sell in the store.

"No," she said suddenly. "Aunt Mildred made it to sell. She would be devastated if she were here, knowing I'd all but talked you out of it."

The way he looked at her made her heart pound. She could see pity written all over his face. If she wasn't careful, she would burst into tears soon. She loved her aunt dearly but hadn't seen her for several months, so it came as a complete surprise when she was notified the store had been left to her in Aunt Mildred's will.

He handed the item over to her, and Ivy instinctively held it against her cheek. "It is so soft and beautiful. Your mother will love this." She glanced up at him and smiled then removed the price tag. "Are you certain? This item is quite expensive – it's…"

He interrupted her. "As I said, no price limit." She nodded and began to fold and box it up.

"Is it her birthday?" she asked curiously. "I might have a gift card. Let me check." She turned her back and rummaged through one of the drawers behind the counter.

"It is," he said to her back.

It wasn't long before she turned back to find him smiling. "Is something funny?" For some reason, he got on her nerves. If she were honest, she'd admit it wasn't for *some reason*. It was because of his comments at the ball. About her eyes having have a mind of their own.

He rubbed his hand across his chin. "I was just thinking about how different you are to the Ivy Henderson I met at the ball." She huffed out a breath of frustration. "It also occurred to me you are very much like your aunt." That she could agree with.

Ivy had spent a lot of time in this little store over the years. Aunt Mildred had bought it after Uncle Henry died some twenty years ago. Aunt Mildred said she needed to do something other than mope around bemoaning the fact her soulmate had passed. And so, this wonderful little store came to life.

Buttons and Bows.

As a young child, and even as a teenager, Ivy often came here for holidays. She helped in the store, and her aunt taught her everything she needed to know to run the place. Little did Ivy know she was grooming her to take over when the inevitable happened.

"Are you all right?" His soft voice cut through her reminiscing, and brought her back to the present.

"What? Oh, sorry. I was thinking about my dear aunt. I'm fine." His hand slipped over hers, and instead of shaking it off, she reveled in his nearness. They'd gotten off on the wrong foot, and Ivy just knew Mildred would be watching over her now and shaking her head at her dislike for the man. It seemed they were friends, after all. Or if not friends, at least strong acquaintances. It would be very wrong of her to continue to hold one mistake against him.

"Are you sure you're fine? I could stay…"

"No, honestly, I'm perfectly fine." She wasn't, but she had no intention of telling him that. She handed him the gift card with flowers printed on it. A perfect match for the gift.

He nodded in acknowledgement then pulled his hand away to take his wallet out of his jacket. She needed to get her mind on the job and finish what she was doing – wrapping this gift for his dear mother.

"Thank you," he said, taking the box from her when she was finished. He nodded then strolled out of the store. Perhaps she'd been too quick to jump to conclusions. He seemed a nice person after all.

Chapter Two

Ivy hurried along to the town hall, pulling her thick coat around her. She'd forgotten how cold it got here in Dewberry. It was even worse on the shopping strip. Dewberry Lane was so sheltered, it barely got much sun, which made it feel even more chilly.

Aunt Mildred had been a staunch supporter of the Christmas Extravaganza, and Ivy felt obligated to do the same. Not that she was sure what would be expected of her. She would be happy to decorate the window of the little store her aunt had named *Buttons and Bows*. Ivy had always felt it a rather strange name for a dress store. It reminded her more of a haberdashery store where you could literally buy buttons and bows. But it was her aunt's store and totally her choice.

At least it *had* been her aunt's store. Now it belonged to Ivy. The thought made her emotional all over again. She'd never planned to move to the beautiful little town of Dewberry. It was so far from civilization, it had not been on Ivy's radar. Not that she was one to go out much. She preferred to sit home at night snuggled under a warm blanket with the fire roaring while winding down from her day.

As a school marm, her days had been busy and often boisterous. It wasn't a vocation she'd chosen; more she'd been finagled into it. When the long-term school marm had become deathly ill, there was no one else to take over. The mayor approached Ivy as the most educated single woman in town, and that was that.

She missed the children for sure, especially little Mary Simpson, who was a hugger. Poor Mary had lost her mother far too soon and needed the comfort of a woman. Her father had tried his best of course, but a young girl needed a mother figure in her life. It had been over three years since his wife passed on, and Mr. Simpson needed to find himself a wife – if only for Mary's sake. Things had looked more promising since Helena Jenkins had come along, which made Ivy feel better about Mary's situation.

Ivy shook herself. Her mind was all over the place since her aunt had passed. Her concentration was shot, and she needed to stop having totally irrelevant thoughts. Finally, she arrived at the town hall, but the door was stuck. She was still trying to move it when Jeremy Hycroft happened along.

"Do you need help, Miss Henderson?"

She stared at him. Was this coincidence, or was he following her? "The door seems to be stuck," she said, wondering if she was being far too suspicious. He was, after all, more than considerate at the store the other day.

"I can't open the door," she said again, feeling rather exasperated as she tried again.

He chuckled. "They reeled you in too? Mildred was always such a great supporter of the Christmas Extravaganza." His eyes sparkled in the moonlight and it lit up his face.

She let out a long breath. "I don't even know what that means."

"The Christmas Extravaganza? I honestly don't think most of us know." Laughing, he pulled out the key and unlocked the door. Ivy stared at him. "Are we the first to arrive?" If that were the case, she shouldn't go inside, shouldn't be alone with Mr. Hycroft. On the other hand, it was beyond cold outside.

"I'm afraid we are. Shall we go inside and get the fire burning? Warm up our frozen bones?"

It made perfect sense to her, although propriety was definitely an issue. "The others should be along shortly." It seemed he could read her thoughts.

He pushed the door open and indicated for her to go ahead, acting like the perfect gentleman. "We meet in the Executive Suite. It is far more comfortable there."

"The Executive Suite?"

He stared momentarily. "Where the Mayor holds meetings and entertains important people. Tonight, we're important." He grinned, and it helped her to relax a little.

They headed up the elegant staircase with its plush carpet of intricate design. The railing was highly polished, and Ivy felt way out of place. She'd never seen anything so precious before. The ballroom was exquisite, but nothing like this.

As they stepped into the Executive Suite, Ivy glanced about. It was expensively furnished, and fitted with padded chairs. On the floor was an expensive rug. Jeremy went directly to the fireplace. It had various sized logs piled next to it and a firebox with twigs and newspaper nearby. He set about lighting the fire while she studied the room.

There was a large mahogany table, where no doubt, countless meetings had been held. It took up a huge chunk of space – more than half the room. On it sat a platter of cheese and crackers and a pitcher of water, along with a number of glasses. Was it for their meeting?

The highbacked chairs had been beautifully upholstered. Ivy hoped she got to sit on them, even if only for a few minutes. She'd never experienced such luxury before.

In the far corner of the enormous room stood a small bar. No doubt there were endless bottles of liquor kept under lock and key. She glanced to the ceiling. The chandelier was more beautiful than anything she'd ever seen and the ceiling beautifully carved. The room screamed of luxury. If it weren't for this meeting, this…Christmas Extravaganza, she would never have had the chance to experience it.

"Do sit down, Miss Henderson." He was still squatting at the fire, and she could see a small flame. Hopefully, it would be roaring soon as the room was rather cold. "The others will be here soon, I'm certain." He glanced over his shoulder at her and grinned. Did he sense how uncomfortable she was feeling, alone with a man she barely knew?

"I'm so sorry," a young woman said as she rushed into the room and pulled off her coat and gloves. "Mr. Hargraves lingered for far too long."

Jeremy smiled at the newcomer. "Of course he did. The poor man is lonely since his wife died, and you are always so kind to him. Ivy Henderson, meet Holly Yates. She owns the *Holly-Berry* cake shop."

He stood, the fire now burning at a good pace. "Miss Henderson has taken over *Buttons and Bows* from Mildred."

Holly raised her eyebrows. "I was sorry to hear about Mildred. What relationship was she to you?"

"Pleased to meet you," Ivy said, nodding at the other woman. "Mildred was my aunt." She hoped she wouldn't have to go through this scenario the entire night. She simply couldn't bear it. "What exactly are we doing here?" she asked pointedly. "The invitation gave no indication."

"And you didn't explain it, Jeremy?" Holly looked slightly annoyed. Was this common place for the only man in the room?

He chuckled. "You are so much better at explaining than I am." He winked at Ivy, and a shiver ran through her. They'd known each other a matter of days. The man had a blasted cheek.

Holly stiffened. "Well then," she said, glaring at the dastardly man. "Every year we hold a Christmas Extravaganza. The aim is to bring more business to Dewberry Lane. We each decorate our stores of course, but there's always more."

She moved closer to the fire and held out her hands, trying to warm them. "Each store has its own in-store Extravaganza, then we finish it off with a bang of some sort."

"What did my aunt do?" She was genuinely curious. What on earth could she do as the dress shop owner?

Holly drew her brows together and tapped her chin.

"I think she ran some knitting sessions last year," Jeremy interrupted.

"Did she?" Holly asked, looking confused.

"I can't even begin to think what I might do," Ivy said, feeling quite deflated. Knitting wasn't even related to a dress shop. She would have to think hard about this.

"The aim is to get *new* customers into our stores. People who have never stepped foot in our doors before."

That was a big ask, especially since Ivy had no idea who had been Aunt Mildred's customers in the past.

It wasn't long before other store owners arrived and the meeting began. They started by introducing themselves since Ivy knew no one. Some she vaguely remembered from her time spent with Aunt Mildred, but most she didn't.

Nothing was achieved except to say they'd meet again next week, hopefully with some ideas. It was frustrating to say the least. Ivy had far too much to do getting the store sorted, not to mention settling into her new home. The apartment above the store was a Godsend. She had no idea where she would be living without it.

If nothing else, she had certainly appreciated the experience of being in this room tonight. It was the most extravagance she'd ever encountered. With the meeting over and the cheese and crackers consumed, everyone piled out of the room and the town hall.

"Might I accompany you home, Miss Henderson?"

It was Jeremy Hycroft. Although she felt a little irritated that he'd withheld information about the Christmas Extravaganza, she was grateful. The last thing she wanted was to walk home in the darkness alone. She hadn't been here in Dewberry long and didn't know her way around. "I thought Dewberry was safe. At least that's what my aunt always told me." She stared at him pointedly, daring him to disagree.

Instead he grinned. "You got me there. It is safe, but I would still rather ensure you got home safely than take the risk of you being harmed by some obnoxious teenage boy with raging hormones."

She was taken aback until she noticed he was still grinning. "Thank you, Mr. Hycroft. I appreciate the gesture."

Now he studied her. "Are we going to continue with formalities? Do call me Jeremy." He paused, and when she didn't answer, continued. "Might I call you Ivy?"

Should she allow it? After all, it seemed Aunt Mildred allowed him to address her by her first name. At least Jeremy had said so.

"I see no harm," she said, then hooked her arm through his. They were the last to leave, and Jeremy locked up the town hall as they left.

"I rather think we could come up with something special for the grand finale this year," he said as they headed down Dewberry Lane.

"We as in you and me, or do you mean the entire committee?" She studied him, but his expression gave nothing away.

"I mean the two of us. That other lot are all about their own stores and nothing else. Whereas you and I are more interested in the entire town. At least I am. What about you?"

She squirmed under his gaze then laughed. "I have only just arrived," she said. "I have no loyalty to this town except the people here loved my aunt and cared for her deeply."

He stopped then and stared at her, raising his eyebrows. "That is very true." He nodded his head then continued to walk. "Out of respect for dear Mildred, I believe we should put our heads together and come up with something spectacular." He blew out a breath as if saying *that's exactly what we need to do.* But was he really thinking of the town, or were his actions more self-centered?

After all, Ivy had absolutely no idea about this man. Nor did she have any inkling of his business.

They walked the rest of the way in silence, and like a real gentleman, he waited until she'd unlocked the door and was safely inside before he left. Despite barely knowing him, Ivy had the distinct feeling he could be trusted.

She stood with her back against the door and listened until she could no longer hear his footsteps as he headed home. It was then she had the strangest feeling. She suddenly missed him.

"Annie!" Jeremy called out to his secretary. "Where are those papers I asked for?" He glanced up to see his long-suffering secretary standing in the doorway, a frustrated look on her face. Mr. Halifax sat opposite; his arthritic hands balanced on the desk waiting to sign the missing paperwork.

Annie took the few steps needed to reach his desk. "Do you mean these papers," she asked, picking up a folder. "The ones I placed right here not twenty minutes ago?" She grinned then headed back to her own desk.

"Ah yes, that's the ones. Thank you, Annie." His mind really wasn't on his work today. Hadn't been since the night of the ball when he'd held Ivy Henderson in his arms. He could try to kid himself and say it was her chameleon eyes that had affected him. But the truth was, the woman herself affected him far more than she should.

He knew if she insisted, the committee would let her out of her Christmas Extravaganza obligation. In fact, a number of them had already told him that was the case, but he would have none of it. Not once he'd met her. Of course, he knew he was being selfish, but he'd used the excuse that Mildred wouldn't be pleased. It made him feel like an utter heel.

Ivy would be quite busy over the coming weeks. Not only did she have to run dear Mildred's store, but she had to unpack her belongings and set up the apartment upstairs. It was a nice little place – Mildred had invited him in for supper on several occasions. It was rather compact, he had to admit that, but it was also homely. At least it was when Mildred lived there.

"Are you all right, Mr. Hycroft?" The elderly man sitting opposite seemed quite concerned when Jeremy glanced up.

"Fine, thank you for asking, Mr. Halifax. I'm a little distracted. I do apologize."

"It's that Christmas Extravaganza thing, isn't it? I don't know why they persist on holding that every year."

Jeremy smiled and handed over the man's new will. "If you would sign here and here," he said, pointing to the places that needed a signature. He blotted the ink and then turned the page. "Only a few more. This one now." Soon they were finished, and he sent the elderly man on his way.

Thank goodness it was almost the end of the day. Perhaps he could drop in and say hello to Miss Henderson. Ivy. Yes, that would be a wonderful way to end a hectic day.

Chapter Three

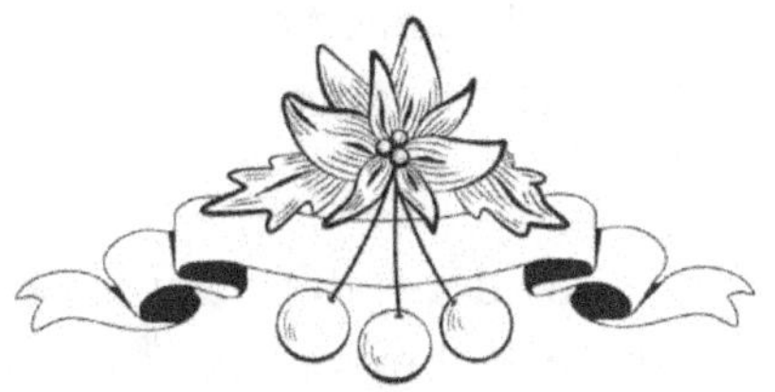

Jeremy added the documents to the safe and tidied up his desk. Tomorrow was another busy day, and he wouldn't have time to clean up in the morning. Besides, Annie would give him an earful for leaving the office in such a mess.

She was a good secretary and had been with him for years. One of these days, his antics would send her packing, and he couldn't abide that happening. She kept him in line, ensured his clients kept coming, and his appointment book was kept in order. He had no idea how or even if he would survive without her.

"Goodnight, Mr. Hycroft," she called from the front office. "I will see you in the morning."

"Yes, goodnight, Annie," he called back. After all these years, she still refused to call him by his Christian name yet insisted he call her Annie. It made no sense, although she'd said it showed respect for his position. He figured it went back to her days with his father. Joshua Hycroft was particularly strict and insisted everyone call him Mr. Hycroft. His demand extended to Jeremy when they were at the office.

He locked his office door, then walked through the waiting area where Annie's desk was located, and finally went outside.

He stared at the words painted in black and gold on the window many years ago – *Hycroft and Son, Solicitors*. Perhaps one day he would have his own son to take over the family business as he had done, but right now, it wasn't something he anticipated. He was after all, thirty-two years old and still unattached. Unless that changed, and soon, there would be no heir. Father would be beyond disgusted with him. The family business had been handed down from his grandfather. Jeremy didn't want to be the one to break the chain of succession, but he really wasn't interested in marriage, let alone children. Jeremy had always enjoyed his bachelor life and the freedoms it allowed him.

He shook himself out of his wayward thoughts and pulled down the shutters, finally locking up for the evening. Jeremy lifted his briefcase from the cobbled path and sighed. Another lonely night at home, and another night of eating alone. He resigned himself to the inevitable then suddenly changed his mind and walked in the opposite direction to his home.

A meal at Ma's Kitchen was exactly what he needed. The food was so good there – just like his own mother used to make. Only it was Merry Jensen's ma who'd originally made the meals, but she was long gone and Merry had taken over. Learning from her mother, Merry's food was every bit as good. His mouth was almost salivating thinking about it, but he still had the same problem – he didn't want to eat alone.

As he strolled past *Buttons and Bows*, he had the perfect solution. He turned back and gazed through the window. He could see Ivy fussing about inside as he guessed she would. The closed sign was on the door, and not one to be easily discouraged, he tapped on the window instead. There was no indication she'd heard, so he tapped a little louder. This time, her head shot up.

"We're closed," she shouted.

"I need to talk to you," he called loudly. He watched as her shoulders sagged and she let out a long breath. It had been a long day and she was probably exhausted. Ivy wasn't used to this sort of work. At least, that's what he figured. She hurried over and unlocked the door.

"Come in," she said quickly, waving him inside, "before someone decides they too need to come in and browse." She looked rather haggard and he worried she was over doing it. "What can I do for you, Mr…er, Jeremy?"

"I'm on my way to Ma's Kitchen and wondered if you would like to accompany me." She looked rather confused, but then her eyes opened wide as if it had suddenly hit her.

"Oh. The diner? Is that what you mean? I probably shouldn't…"

"You haven't eaten yet, I presume?" He glanced at his pocket watch. The store wouldn't have been closed terribly long. Surely, she hadn't eaten already?

"No. No, I haven't. Only I hadn't expected to eat out tonight."

On closer inspection, she really did look drained.

"My treat. What I really wanted was some company, and I thought you could do with a break from all this." He spread his arms wide and glanced about.

"Thank you," she said quietly. "That would be lovely. I need to run upstairs and get my coat first."

She scurried off and he waited patiently. He really was looking forward to dining with the delightful Ivy Henderson.

They were seated at a table by the window. It was the owner herself who waited on them, Jeremy explained. Normally, she would have staff taking care of customers, but being mid-week, it was quiet, so most likely, she would be alone.

"Nice to see you, Jeremy," she said, glancing at Ivy curiously.

"Hello, Merry. This is Ivy Henderson, Mildred's niece."

"I was sorry to hear about Mildred's passing," Merry said gently. "She was a wonderful person." She handed them each a menu then disappeared before Ivy had a chance to respond.

"Everyone loved Mildred," he explained. "Her loss has been felt by a lot of people, but no more than you, I'm sure." He reached across the table and covered her hand.

Ivy glanced down. Should she wrench her hand away? She really should, but it was comforting.

"I apologize," Jeremy hurriedly said. "I had no right to take liberties." He looked every bit as apologetic as he sounded.

She smiled tentatively. "You were trying to console, so I don't mind in this instance." Was he though? The thought suddenly struck her. She shook it off equally as quick.

Merry returned and they gave their orders. "Have you thought any more about what you're doing for the extravaganza?"

He studied her, and it made Ivy feel a little uneasy. "I haven't. You?" It suddenly occurred to her that she had no idea what he did for a living. "What is your occupation, anyway?" She didn't mean to but totally blurted the words out.

His reaction was to grin. "I'm a solicitor," he said, straightening his tie as though a perfect tie proved his point. "I have this same dilemma every year. I honestly don't know why I bother, but Annie makes me."

Annie? His wife? Or a girlfriend? "And who might this *Annie* be?" Why did she even care?

He grinned again. "My secretary. She does all the business side of things, while I get to do all the boring stuff." He grimaced and it made her laugh.

"It really isn't funny," he said, still scowling. "It's far from laughable. My job is rather tedious – there's no other way to put it."

"What? You don't enjoy writing wills? I'd have thought that rather exciting," she said, a tinge of sarcasm in her voice.

He smirked then. "You're a real card," he said mildly. "The only thing I enjoy is that I know what people will get when someone drops off the earth, before the recipient does." Now he grinned.

It was about then Merry brought their food to the table. "It smells divine, Merry," Ivy said, leaning over the food to better experience the aroma. "Thank you."

"Yes, thank you, Merry. It smells quite delicious."

Jeremy picked up his fork but was interrupted. "You don't bless your food?" Ivy inquired, rather taken aback.

He floundered then and replaced the cutlery on the table. "Of course, but I wasn't sure if you did." He reached out for her hand. "Bless this food, Lord, and also this new friendship. Amen."

She smiled. Jeremy was right – they were friends. They'd become friends very quickly, which was pleasing since she really didn't know anyone else in town. Not really.

The lamb roast was delicious, and apparently Jeremy thought so too as he made short work of his food. "Merry is an excellent cook," he said as he wiped his mouth with the linen cloth.

Ivy took a sip of water. "She certainly is. I'll have to keep this place in mind for the future."

"Aren't you glad you came tonight?" Without giving her a chance to respond, he changed the subject entirely. "What *are* you doing for the extravaganza? Any ideas about our finale?"

For a moment, she was confused. She hadn't expected to be bombarded with questions. Nor had she thought much about the Christmas Extravaganza. She'd been far too busy trying to sort out the store. Aunt Mildred had been quite ill near the end, and unable to do much. If only she'd let Ivy know, she could have come far sooner.

"I…I really don't know. It's not that long since the meeting. What about you? Any suggestions at all?"

He chuckled. "I always leave the ideas to Annie. Mostly, she arranges little lectures about why it's important to have a current will." He pulled a face. "Of course, I'm the one who has to deliver the information."

"Oh, that sounds excellent." And it did. Ivy thought that a wonderful idea, and wondered how many people didn't have a will when they died. "I've really not thought about it much, with so much unpacking and rearranging to do. I still have a few weeks – don't I?" She chewed on her bottom lip with worry. What if she had to make a decision at next week's meeting?

Merry removed their soiled dishes. "Did you want dessert?"

"Silly question," Jeremy said, a smile on his face. "Since when have I *not* had dessert?"

Merry grinned too. "Since never. Tonight's selection is peach cobbler, apple cinnamon muffin, and blueberry pie."

"Sounds lovely. I'll have peach cobbler, please." Ivy didn't often have dessert but didn't want to feel out of place since Jeremy would be ordering.

"I'll have the same, thanks. Both with clotted cream please, Merry." He winked at their hostess. Was there something between them? Well, if there was, it was not Ivy's business. She and Jeremy were nothing more than friends. Acquaintances. They'd only met a short time ago, so she wasn't sure why she felt a stab of jealously. It was absolutely ludicrous, particularly when she had no interest in Jeremy except as a friend.

They finished off dessert with a mug of coffee, then Jeremy walked her home. "I had a very enjoyable evening," he said when they were standing outside her apartment. "Thank you for agreeing to accompany me. We shall have to do it again sometime."

She stared at him. Did he think this was a date? That he was courting her? She mentally shook herself. That was probably the last thing on his mind. It was simply as he'd told her when he invited her to eat with him. He didn't want to eat alone.

So why did she feel there was something more between them? "Thank you, Jeremy. I had a lovely time too." If they were simply friends, why did she have a hollow feeling when he said goodnight and turned to leave?

Ivy shook herself mentally. She had arrived in a new town only weeks ago and had no other friends. Of course, that was the reason. She was still adapting to living here and knowing few people. That's all there was to it.

She was determined to convince herself that was the crux of the matter.

Chapter Four

Ivy was beginning to panic.

The next committee meeting for the extravaganza was scheduled for later that evening. She still had no idea what she would do for her part in it, and they would be sure to ask. What on earth could she do that wouldn't jeopardize sales in her little store? And what about the finale? Jeremy was counting on her to come up with a fresh idea.

She stood at the stand where the undergarments were kept and folded them back to their original state. It was not something Aunt Mildred sold, but Ivy thought it might be a nice little side-line. That way, her customers could buy the majority of their requirements right here at *Buttons and Bows*. It would help the customers as well as her profit margin.

Of course, she kept them in out of sight near the back of the store. Heaven forbid the husband of one of her customers accompany his wife inside. Having bloomers, petticoats, corsets, and chemise in full sight simply wouldn't do.

The nightgowns were nearby as well, although, they weren't as sensitive as the other items. They were all new additions, and before she'd ordered them, Ivy wondered how well they would sell. She'd ordered them almost as soon as she'd arrived in Dewberry since it was rather isolated and would take some time to arrive.

She'd purchased a selection of cotton and silk. The more prominent women in town went straight for the silk undergarments, as she'd expected. But she sold far more of the more practical cotton garments.

Already, word had got around, and she'd had some rather embarrassed gentlemen looking for a special gift for their wives. She assured them she was discreet about her customer's purchases. It alerted Ivy to the fact she should perhaps order in a few of the more risqué items. *Kept under the counter, of course.* What married couples did in their own home was none of her business. Still, it brought a smile to her face.

The bell on the door jingled and she glanced up. It wouldn't be long before it would be time to close the store for the evening. "Good evening, Mrs. Grayson. What might I do for you today?"

The older woman fiddled about with her gloves, pulling them off and shaking out the snow. "Brrrr, it is quite chilly outside," she said as she removed her coat. Was she in for the long haul? Ivy hoped not. "I heard you'd acquired some new items for your store," she said as she winked. "I know you're being very discreet about it, but…"

She let the word hang, and Ivy immediately knew what her best customer wanted. By this time, she had moved to the front of the store and taken Mrs. Grayson's coat from her and hung it up. "If you'll follow me, I do believe I know what you're looking for."

"It's lovely and warm in here, my dear. I am pleased you keep that fire going. It was too much for your dear aunt in the end, and it was near to freezing in here at times."

"I do wish she'd sent for me," Ivy said, meaning every word. "I only discovered the situation when she'd already passed."

Mrs. Grayson stared at her. "You weren't close then?" She looked rather confused since Aunt Mildred had left the store to Ivy.

"We *were* close," she said. "Very close, in fact. We corresponded regularly, and I'd received a letter from her not a week earlier. She made no mention of any illness."

Mrs. Grayson pursed her lips. "That was very naughty of our dear Mildred. She'd been struggling for quite some time. At least a couple of months. She even got one of the local women to help her with the store when it all became too much."

Ivy swallowed. She'd been here earlier in the year. Why hadn't she noticed?

"It came on rather abruptly," Mrs. Grayson said. "She seemed perfectly fine one day, then deathly ill the next. The doctor said it was her heart and would one day stop without warning." She reached out and took Ivy's hand. "That's exactly what happened," she said quietly. Tears formed in the woman's eyes. "I don't think I'll ever forget it. I'd made a purchase the previous day, and when I came to collect it the next morning, there she was – dead on the floor." Tears rolled down her face, and Ivy pulled her into an embrace.

"Oh, my gosh," Ivy said quietly, trying to hold back her own tears. "I had no idea. I'm so sorry you had to endure that, Mrs. Grayson." She rubbed a hand over the woman's back, trying to console her. Suddenly, she pulled herself out of Ivy's arms and composed herself, as though nothing had ever happened.

"Thank you, but I am fine. It was nothing compared to what our dear Mildred endured." She swiped at her face and straightened her shoulders. "Shall we check out the undergarments," Mrs. Grayson demanded, successfully changing the subject to one less morbid.

She followed Ivy to the back of the store, her eyes checking out each and every display stand. "Oh, you have nightgowns as well. I shall need to check those out too." She stared at Ivy momentarily. "You are clever. Everything in one store." Mrs. Grayson grinned. "I'm surprised Mildred didn't think of it. She was quite the businesswoman, your aunt."

"She truly was," Ivy said. She'd spent enough time in this store over the years, and had watch her aunt with customers. A gentle suggestion here and there often doubled her profits. She was quite cunning too. It was very obvious now she'd been training Ivy for the inevitable. She'd summoned her to Dewberry every time the opportunity arose. Every school holiday, Ivy would spend the majority of her time in the store with Aunt Mildred. She'd enjoyed every minute of it.

When she'd arrived this time, she wasn't walking into a totally new environment. Nor did she arrive to run a business she knew nothing about. Yes, her aunt really was quite astute.

"Have you decided what you'll do for the Christmas Extravaganza," Mrs. Grayson suddenly asked as they neared the undergarments.

Ivy screwed up her face. "It is the bane of my existence right now," she said, feeling rather stressed about the entire situation. "Surely, they could have given me a pass this year." It was a statement rather than a question.

"Would you have wanted that? I doubt Mildred would be pleased," the elderly woman went on to say. "She built up a lovely business for your inheritance. I'd hate to think of her being let down." Ivy could see exactly what she was doing. Dear Mrs. Grayson was trying to guilt her into joining the extravaganza. "It's a tradition on Dewberry Lane, and Mildred was part of that tradition for as long as she owned the store. Decades." She stared at Ivy with beady eyes that said *I'll guilt you into this if that's what it takes.*

"You are right. Of course, I owe Aunt Mildred that much. The trouble is, I have absolutely no idea what to do." She held up a striking pair of silk bloomers, and Mrs. Grayson nodded her agreement. "She must have been running out of ideas herself if she resorted to knitting lessons last year."

"I'll take three of those, my dear." She checked out the remaining undergarments and handed Ivy her selections. All ten of them. "By the way, that is utter nonsense about the knitting lessons. Who told you that?" She studied Ivy for a moment or two. "Oh, I know. It was Jeremy Hycroft. The man wouldn't have a clue."

She moved to the table with the nightgowns. Ivy was relieved she had stocked items suitable for larger figures. Mrs. Grayson could be described as rather stocky, but she bought only the best available. "Mildred ran classes on how to choose garments that flattered whatever figure you might have been blessed with."

"That sounds lovely," Ivy said, showing the woman several different nightgowns, hoping at least one appealed to her.

"All of those, thank you, dear," Mrs. Grayson said with satisfaction. "Put them on my account, and I'll collect them all tomorrow if that suits."

"I can deliver them to your home if that suits you better." She was more than happy to deliver them. Ethel Grayson was her best customer and had been her aunt's as well.

"Goodness no, but thank you." She looked taken aback. "My visits to Dewberry Lane are the highlight of my week." She glanced at Ivy, a smile on her face, and Ivy was convinced what she said was true.

She glanced at the clock on the wall behind the counter. "I mustn't keep you any longer. You have a committee meeting tonight."

Ivy didn't need reminding. Once again, she would turn up with no ideas whatsoever. What would everyone else think of her? She dared not even wonder. She glanced up as the bell over the door jingled. Jeremy Hycroft stood there with the door wide open.

"Do close the door, Mr. Hycroft," Mrs. Grayson called out. "You are letting all the warmth out." She turned to Ivy. "You be careful of that young man," she said quietly. "He's on the lookout for a wife, I hear." She winked. "He needs an heir, you know."

Ivy shuddered. "Well, he can look elsewhere," she said. "I am not interested in marrying. Nor am I interested in providing heirs to anyone. Especially Mr. Hycroft. He can be quite rude at times."

Her customer sighed. "Young men are not what they used to be," the older woman said, reaching out to touch Ivy's hand. "You watch yourself."

Ivy held back a grin and walked her to the front door, then helped Mrs. Grayson into her coat. "Enjoy your meeting," she said as she walked out the door. Ivy sensed sarcasm in her words.

"What can I do for you, Jeremy," Ivy said with some skepticism. "I need to sort this lot out then prepare for the meeting."

"Good evening, Ivy," he said as though she hadn't spoken a word. "I've come to take you to Ma's

Kitchen. I thought we could have a light supper before the meeting."

Did he indeed? Was Mrs. Grayson right to warn her about Jeremy Hycroft and his need for an heir? With the thought now planted in her mind, Ivy would be far more wary of the handsome young man standing opposite her.

"We both need to eat," he said as he studied her. He was right. They needed to fuel their bodies to endure the torture that came disguised as a committee meeting.

"Yes, we do. Give me a moment to sort this lot out, and I'll run upstairs for my coat." She turned to the door and flipped over the closed sign, locking the door as she did. "I do not want any more customers tonight. Mrs. Grayson is an exception." Ivy was certain every one of the business owners would feel the same.

She took all of Mrs. Grayson's purchases and placed them underneath the counter. That would be her first task for the morning.

She left Jeremy staring after her as she went upstairs to collect her warm coat.

As they walked toward the town hall, Jeremy slipped his arm into Ivy's. After what Mrs. Grayson had told her about Jeremy Hycroft requiring an heir, she would be more cautious around him. "Where is your office located," she asked as they strolled past *Buttons and Bows* after they'd left *Ma's Kitchen.*

He indicated further down along Dewberry Lane. "It's a little further past the town hall."

"I'd love to see it now, if we have the time."

Jeremy pulled out his pocket watch then glanced up at her. "Provided we don't dally, we could do that," he said. "You won't see much though. The shutters are pulled down every evening."

"Bother," Ivy said more vigorously than she'd intended. "Perhaps some other time then."

"Perhaps," he said, then led her toward the town hall door.

"I did have a bit of a thought," she said, glancing across at him. "About this big finale you keep going on about."

He stopped dead, almost tripping her over as his arm was linked through hers. "Go on…"

She studied him momentarily then licked her lips. "This might be a moot point, since you might already do it."

Jeremy frowned. "Do continue, Ivy. I am tense with anticipation."

His words made her laugh. "Well," she said as she closed her eyes in thought. Perhaps it wasn't that good an idea after all? "What about a Christmas tree?"

He stared at her then, his expression one of disappointment. "Most of the stores already have a Christmas tree." He turned away from her then and began to walk toward the town hall again.

"Honestly, Jeremy," she said in an exasperated tone. "That's not what I meant."

"Oh?" He stopped again, but this time, it wasn't quite so abruptly, ensuring she didn't almost trip again.

So now he was interested. She was beginning to see why Mrs. Grayson had little time for him. "I am talking about a giant tree, right in the middle of Dewberry Lane." She indicated the area where she thought it could be placed. "Everyone in town could help to decorate it, and there could be a box for toy donations – for less fortunate children." She glanced at him, raising her eyebrows in question. "Perhaps even food donations."

"I say," Jeremy said, wholly animated. "That could work. The whole idea of the extravaganza is to get people to Dewberry Lane. If they buy things to donate – that's even better."

That wasn't really what she had in mind, but no matter.

He hooked his arm in hers again, and they were once more on their way. With so many stop-starts, it felt like the longest walk she'd ever taken along this shopping strip. It almost made her chuckle.

When they arrived at the town hall, Jeremy pulled out his key and led her inside. As they went upstairs, she didn't feel anywhere near as uncomfortable as last time. Likely because she'd gotten to know Jeremy Hycroft, and felt she could trust him.

They entered the Executive Suite, only this time, she didn't spend so much time glancing about. Although, she did feel more inclined to touch the surfaces and bend down and run her hands over the luxurious carpet. It was every bit as splendid as she'd thought last time.

Jeremy had the fire burning wonderfully as the other committee members began to stream through the door.

"Ivy has had the most wonderful idea," Jeremy blurted out as everyone arrived. She felt heat creep up her face and moved closer to the now roaring fire to try and cover her embarrassment. That way, everyone might think her cheeks were pink from the heat. At least she hoped they did.

"Tell us," they all said at once.

Jeremy held up his palm to them. "You need to wait until the meeting begins," he said. It looked suspiciously as though he was trying to force back a grin. Ivy couldn't help but smile. He really was a tease.

"Well, that's not fair," Belle Armstrong from *Candies Galore* said. "Shall we start the meeting now?"

Noelle Jenkins from *Book Time* added her opinion. "I think we should."

Everyone sat at the large mahogany table Ivy had admired so much last time, and a hearty discussion began.

Chapter Five

"I hear last night's meeting went well," Mrs. Grayson said as she breezed through the front door.

Ivy rushed over to help her best customer out of her coat. "Is it snowing? I had no idea," she said as she brushed a small amount of snow from Mrs. Grayson's coat and hung it up.

"It's not heavy, not yet. But you mark my words. With only a matter of weeks until Christmas, it will get far heavier than it is right now." She nodded assuredly, and Ivy had no doubt she was correct.

"Aunt Mildred hated the snow," Ivy reminisced. "I remember one year I arrived only days after

Christmas, and she was still bemoaning the snow." It was only one of many wonderful memories Ivy had of her dear aunt.

She startled when Mrs. Grayson reached out and rubbed a hand up Ivy's arm. "She was a wonderful woman, our Mildred. We spent Christmas together most years. Did you know that?" She looked up at Ivy expectantly. "I suppose you didn't know we were friends."

Ivy swallowed. She didn't, but she should have. Aunt Mildred rarely wrote about herself in her correspondence. She mostly talked about the store and Dewberry itself.

"No, of course you didn't," Mrs. Grayson suddenly said. "Mildred was far too private for that." She fiddled with her scarf for a moment then suddenly pulled it off. "Do you have my purchases ready?"

"Of course," Ivy said as she reached underneath the counter and pulled out a large box. She'd tied it with an oversized bow, making it look more like a gift than something her customer had brought for herself. "My offer still stands," she said. "I am more than happy to deliver this to your home."

"Fiddlesticks!" Mrs. Grayson waved her hands about as though she'd been scalded. "And deprive me of the opportunity to come to town and indulge myself with more purchases?" She suddenly reached into her reticule and pulled out her pocketbook.

She handed Ivy a wad of notes. "Put that toward my account. I must owe a substantial amount by now. I was about to top it up when dear Mildred…" She stopped herself short and pursed her lips.

Ivy took the bundle of notes, but balked at the amount. "That is far too much, Mrs. Grayson, surely?"

"If it's too much, put it toward future purchases. You know there will be more," she said, winking conspiratorially at Ivy. "This is my favorite store in town," she said, then suddenly turned away and headed for the door.

Ivy hurried after her with Mrs. Grayson's box of purchases. "You forgot this," she said as her customer opened the door. "Oh, and your coat."

As she helped the older lady into her luxurious coat, Ivy noticed the expensive looking carriage sitting a short way from *Buttons and Bows*. The exterior was made of leather of the best quality and had been kept in excellent condition. The driver stood waiting patiently next to the carriage. Several packages were tied on the roof; his passenger had likely collected them along the way.

As Mrs. Grayson got closer, he stepped toward her and took the package from Ivy. Putting it aside, he handed his passenger into the carriage then secured the package with the others. He tipped his hat at her then mounted the buggy himself. It was then Ivy realized Mrs. Grayson was far better off than she had ever envisioned.

Still stunned by the revelation, Ivy made her way inside. She checked the clock behind the counter – it was nearly time for a break. She hurried to the fire and threw on some more logs, since it was rather cold outside with the snow being relatively heavy today. The last thing she needed was for her customers to complain about the temperature inside her store.

The fire was warming, and she lingered longer than she should have. Going out in the cold without a coat was foolish. She needed to ensure she didn't do it again.

The bell over the door jingled. "I could have done that for you," a familiar voice called out. Ivy stood then sighed. Was the implication she was incapable of lighting a fire or keeping it going because she was a woman? She certainly hoped not.

"Good morning, Jeremy," she called grimly as she turned to face him.

He pulled out his pocket watch. "Actually," he said, glancing down at it, "it's past midday. Would you indulge a boring solicitor and join me for a bite to eat?"

She glanced up at the clock. He was correct. Where on earth had the morning gone? Mrs. Grayson liked to hang around and talk, but it didn't bother Ivy. The woman was such a joy. Not to mention she was a friend of Aunt Mildred's. "I'm not sure…"

"You have to eat," he said, pouting like a small child. It made her laugh. "What, might I ask, do you find so funny?" His expression was blank, so Ivy had no idea if he was joking or not.

She frowned at him. "If only you could have seen your face." She laughed again, and this time he joined her.

"Is that a yes?" He was determined, there was no doubt about it. "I had Merry make up some sandwiches and cake. I hope you don't mind?"

He studied her, and she could see he had already decided. The man was rather pushy, but he was growing on her. "What did you have in mind?"

"A walk along Dewberry Lane – that way you can see where my office is – and then we could take a stroll through the park."

"Sounds lovely." She wasn't sure it did, but she had no intention of being rude to the man. He had, after all, invited her to lunch and gone to some expense to do it.

"I thought we could sit in the pergola. It would protect us from the weather, and you would get to see more of Dewberry."

She stared at him. Did he not realize she'd been coming here for years? No matter, it did sound like a lovely way to spend her break.

"Well? What do you think? Ivy?" He reached over and touched her arm. "Are you all right? You seemed to zoom out for a while there." When she glanced at him, he seemed quite concerned, which sent warmth down her spine.

"Sorry," she said, shaking herself. "I was thinking about Aunt Mildred. I believe she took me to the park once, many years ago." He looked disappointed so she set about reassuring him. "I don't recall a pergola though."

He brightened up then. "It's a new addition, although, I believe it's been there for three years at least. Off you go then," he said in his pushy way. "Grab your coat and we'll be off."

When she glanced back, he was wearing a massive grin. Mrs. Grayson's words echoed in her mind. The last thing she wanted was to become Jeremy's wife as a way of giving him heirs.

"As much as I've enjoyed our little outing," Ivy said, brushing the crumbs from her skirt, "I really must get back to the store. "With any luck, I'll have customers lined up outside trying to get in." She grinned then, knowing it was highly unlikely.

"Wouldn't that be nice?" Apart from being thoroughly pushy and making insolent comments about her changing eye color, Jeremy had been a perfect gentleman. If Mrs. Grayson hadn't made remarks about him wanting an heir, Ivy might find herself warming to the man. She may even consider allowing him to court her. If he'd asked, that was.

Goodness, she was getting way too far ahead of herself. Besides, she was not anyone's heir receptacle. Ivy shook herself inwardly. Her thoughts were spinning out of control.

They stood almost at the same moment, and he reached out to take her rubbish. Their hands brushed and a tingle ran up her arm. She stared down at their hands.

"I say, Ivy," he said quietly. "You're a little out of it today. Are you sure you're okay?"

He looked rather concerned, and it bothered her that she'd caused him anxiety. "I think I'm still in shock over Aunt Mildred." She glanced up at him and saw pity on his face. "You'd think by now…"

"It takes time," he said gently, reaching for her hands. He shoved the rubbish into his suit pocket and pulled her down to sit again. "Especially when it's unexpected."

He held both her hands in a light grip. Was this his solicitor voice? Or was he truly being her friend. "Aunt Mildred was the last family I had left," she said as an errant tear rolled down her cheek. She quickly wiped it away.

Ivy abruptly stood. "I'm sorry," she said. "I didn't mean to pile my worries onto you." She turned away and wiped at her face again, finally containing her emotions. "We should go."

Without giving him a choice, she began to walk hurriedly back toward Dewberry Lane. "Ivy." His voice was urgent, yet gentle. She stopped abruptly and turned to face him. Jeremy's arms were outstretched, and there was no denying she wanted to be enveloped in them. But should she allow herself this indulgence?

"You're upset," he said quietly. "Let me console you." She stepped into his arms and immediately felt better. Despite the relatively short time they'd known each other, Jeremy had become a dear friend, a confidante of sorts. Standing there in his embrace made her feel all sorts of things, comforted was definitely one of them.

Her tears began to fall once more, and as much as she tried to hold them back, they continued to tumble down her cheeks. He rubbed his hands across her back and it helped. "Feel any better?" he asked tenderly. "Crying can often help, you know. But you've probably done more than your fair share of crying since Mildred passed."

She pulled back abruptly and stared at him. "No. No, I haven't. This is the first time I've cried since she passed." She sniffed then pulled a handkerchief from her reticule and wiped at her face. "I must look an absolute mess," she said, turning her face away.

"You look perfectly fine," he said gently. "A little flushed perhaps."

He was being kind. No, he was being polite. Ivy knew her eyes would be red and puffy and her face bright red, not to mention her nose would be glowing. What a disaster.

"Is it terrible to hope there's not a queue of ladies waiting at the door?" She managed a tight smile and he laughed. It was just what she needed.

"You are such a gem," he told her. "There's a water fountain a little way from here if you'd like to stop there before we return." Without waiting for a reply, he guided her toward it and stood back while she splashed water over her face. It felt wonderful, soothing even, but she felt nothing but total embarrassment at her outpouring of emotions.

"I think I'm ready," she said quietly.

He studied her momentarily then reached out and pushed a stray tuft of hair back off her face. His fingers caressed her face, and a shiver went through her. Ivy sighed and stared into his eyes. He did the same.

"What color are they now?" she asked quietly.

"Green, like the grass we are standing on." He continued to stare but didn't remove his hand from her cheek. "Ivy…" he began, but she interrupted him.

"We should get back."

But he had other ideas and leaned in and kissed her. She might not have minded any other time, but why did he have to pick right now when she was an absolute disaster?

When she thought about it, she probably would mind at another time too. She didn't want to get married. Not to Jeremy, and not to anyone else. Not now anyway.

What she really needed to do was stop letting her mind run wild. She needed to think about the kiss instead. She closed her eyes and leaned into him. His arms slid up around her, and he pulled her closer. This time was different to the last time he held her. He was trying to console her earlier. This time was something else entirely and was really nice.

Suddenly, he stepped back. "I apologize," he said hastily, straightening his jacket. "I had no right. Especially after you'd been so upset." He ran his hands over his chin. "I feel as though I've taken advantage of your state of mind."

"If anyone has taken advantage, it's me," she said firmly. "I'm the one who had an emotional outburst. I'm sorry for taking advantage of your friendship." She felt truly bad.

"Shall we agree to disagree then?" He slipped his arm through hers and they headed back to *Buttons and Bows*.

Her aim had been to distance herself from Jeremy Hycroft, but their encounter today had brought them even closer. The last thing she needed was a relationship. Not that he'd mentioned such a word, but that kiss… it felt like the beginning of the very thing she was trying to avoid.

"Ah, you see," he said as they almost reached her store. "No gabble of ladies to notice your puffy eyes."

She glared at him. "You said I looked fine."

"And you do. I was endeavoring to cheer you up."

Ivy pouted. "Well, it didn't work." She pulled out her keys and unlocked the door. "Thank you for everything," she said. "Next time, it's my shout for lunch or supper, or whatever."

He suddenly grinned. "Supper tonight. Wonderful. Shall I make a booking at Ma's Kitchen?" His expression was teasing, but she knew he wasn't teasing about supper. Strangely, enough she was looking forward to it. Perhaps, like Jeremy, she no longer wanted to dine alone.

She nodded and he grinned. "Good. I'll pick you up at six." He leaned in and gave her a quick kiss on the cheek then was suddenly gone. She brought her hand up to her cheek and covered the place he'd kissed her. It was still tingling when she could no longer see him along the strip. Ivy wasn't sure what to make of it.

Chapter Six

"I've had a few thoughts," Ivy said, wiping her mouth with the linen napkin.

Jeremy raised his eyebrows. "Are you talking about the extravaganza, or is that in regard to me courting you?"

Now it was her turn to raise her eyebrows. "What?" She sputtered, momentarily taken aback. Jeremy could be funny when he wanted to be. "Oh, I get it. That's a joke. Right?" Suddenly she wasn't quite so sure.

He tried to force back a smile, but she saw it, and challenged him on it. "So, it was a joke?" One part of her was disappointed. The other part, she wasn't so sure. She really like Jeremy, and he seemed to like her – and not just as a way to bear his children either, as Mrs. Grayson had suggested.

He lifted his napkin and rubbed it across his mouth. "Why would you even think that?" He suddenly appeared disappointed. "You know I have a real fondness for you, Ivy."

Well, now she knew where she stood. Jeremy had finally declared his feelings. He had a *fondness* for her. That wasn't the same as falling in love, or even thinking you might be in love. Fondness was more along the lines you'd expect with friends.

"I'm sure you do," she said, tossing her napkin on the table.

He stared at her then frowned so hard his eyebrows were almost joined.

"Is something wrong?"

"Wrong? No, of course not," she almost snarled. He reached across the table and covered her hand.

"You seem…upset. Did I say something out of place?" He genuinely didn't know. That was even worse.

If he truly only felt fondness for Ivy, why did he kiss her? Why did he hold her in his arms the way he did? And why did he insist on spending time with her every chance he got? The trouble was, she was falling for him, and if he didn't feel the same, she needed to break ties. She needed to not dine with him again, not go for strolls in the park, and needed to never see him again.

That really cut through her heart. She'd become far more than fond of Jeremy Hycroft, but now it was time to stand back, to keep her distance. With desert over, there was no reason to stay. The sooner she broke those ties with him, the better. Her heart thudded. The thought made her feel ill and she felt the color drain from her face.

"I…I need to go home," she said quietly. "I suddenly feel very unwell."

He stared into her face. "You are quite pale." He lifted his arm to summon the waitress over then pulled some notes from his wallet.

"It was meant to be my treat tonight," she said, opening her reticule.

He chuckled. "That was never going to happen. Did you honestly think I would let you pay?"

She should have known, and she really should protest, but she didn't have the energy right now. The shock of knowing Jeremy had played her, kissed her with no intention of following through, had really stung. She was just a pawn in his silly games.

Ivy began to stand, and he was quickly by her side. An arm around her waist to support her, they left

Ma's Kitchen. "I, don't know what came over me," she said quietly. "I was fine, and then I wasn't." She glanced up into his face, and he looked truly worried for her.

"Should I call the doctor?" Concern was etched all over his face. That was the last thing she wanted. He was her friend, after all. At least, he was now. But once all ties were broken…She couldn't bear the thought.

"I'll be fine," she said, forcing herself to smile. "I'm probably just tired."

He nodded but she wasn't sure he believed her. "I'll call around in the morning to check on you."

She sighed. That was just like Jeremy, good friend that he was. "Thank you, but there's no need." He took the key when they arrived at the store and unlocked the door. "I'll see you upstairs," he said gently. "I'd hate for you to fall and I was none the wiser."

Now it was her turn to nod. No matter what she said, he would insist, so she might as well agree. Her heart was shattered. Not that she'd wanted anything romantic with Jeremy, but she couldn't allow him to kiss her then decide he was only fond of her. That would never do.

He saw her upstairs and promised to lock up on his way out. He still looked quite concerned when he left.

Ivy felt awful. Had she led him on? She didn't think so, but what if she had? Then it was all on her. She had no experience with men and had no idea how to play their silly games. Why couldn't they just come out and say what they meant instead of beating around the bush?

She climbed into bed and fell asleep almost the moment her head hit the pillow.

Morning came far too quickly, and Ivy sat in her tiny kitchen drinking tea and contemplating her day. She needed to check the stock today. She'd have to place an order with her supplier in the next two days or wait a month before the next delivery.

Aunt Mildred, angel that she was, had made a list of her suppliers, delivery times, and more. It would be a huge help, and Ivy would be forever grateful. The worst part was Aunt Mildred definitely knew she wouldn't be around much longer. Ivy deeply regretted the fact she hadn't known. She'd carried on with her own life as though nothing was amiss. As though Aunt Mildred wasn't dying. Her heart was heavy, and she felt responsible for not being around when her aunt needed her the most.

Time was ticking away, and she needed to open the store shortly. Ivy finished up her tea and went to the bathroom to freshen up before going downstairs. Her hair was still hanging down her back, so she twisted it and fashioned it at the back of her head. She splashed water in her face as well, to ensure she was properly awake. She still felt a little unwell, but she had far too much to do today. Sickness could find somewhere else to live.

Once ready, she unlocked the door to the private residence and went downstairs. There was a cluster of at least six ladies standing at the door waiting to come in. She checked the clock over the counter. There was still ten minutes before the store was due to open. What was going on?

She'd planned to do a little stock checking before the opening time, but it wasn't to be. She hastily moved to the front door and unlocked it. Jeremy had secured the store as he'd promised he would. Ivy was certain she could rely on him.

"Good morning, ladies," she said cheerfully. "I haven't even lit the fire yet." She raised an eyebrow in question. But no one said a word. They suddenly rushed past her, and straight to the back of the store. She quickly understood. Mrs. Grayson had spread word of her new supplies. Her undergarments.

She squatted down to light the fire but was immediately summoned for assistance. "Could you help me with sizing," Mrs. Halicourt asked.

"Me too," said Mrs. Jolimont.

"Oh, I must check those nightgowns," Mrs. Herbert said as she rushed toward that particular table.

Ivy was dizzy with excitement. This was exactly what she'd wanted, and Mrs. Grayson had made it happen. She rushed over to her customers – the fire would have to wait. The bell over the door jingled and she looked up. Jeremy Hycroft. Well he did say he'd call in and check on her.

"Good morning, ladies," he said with a grin on his face. "My gosh, it's cold in here," he said, exaggerating at shivering.

"Sorry," she called across the room. "I haven't had a chance to light it yet. These ladies were waiting out in the cold wanting to come in."

He didn't say another word, but rushed toward the fireplace. This was exactly what he wanted, and Ivy felt like she'd played right into his hands. She believed his opinion of women lighting fires was they were doing men's work. It still irked her. Despite that, she was grateful of his assistance this morning.

She glanced up as the bell jingled yet again. This time, she was prepared for the onslaught and helped the ladies out of their warm coats. "Good morning, ladies," she said pleasantly. "Is there something in particular I can help you with?"

Mrs. Jacobsen leaned forward and whispered in her ear. Ivy pointed toward the back where the other ladies were rifling through the stands of undergarments. "Do let me know if I can help anyone," she said as she approached them.

Jeremy stood and brushed the dust off his clothes then turned to her. She heard the collective gasp as he headed her way. That would never do. She signaled for him to go in the other direction. She didn't want to lose her customers who'd shown more enthusiasm today than they'd ever shown.

He waited at the front counter. "Thank you for lighting the fire," she said quietly. "I do appreciate it. It's just…" She stared at him, not wanting to say the words.

"I understand. We won't mention the unmentionables." He laughed, but Ivy didn't think it was funny. "I came to check on you. There's some color in your cheeks this morning. Are you feeling any better?"

She felt terrible. She'd caused him worry, and she deeply regretted it. "It's strange. I am perfectly fine today. Thank you for checking on me."

"But you want me to leave you and your unmentionable ladies alone." She couldn't help but laugh. It really was quite funny, even if it was rather wicked.

"That would be lovely. Oh, not that I'm trying to get rid of you. And I do appreciate the fire…" Even Ivy knew she was babbling. Anything to avoid talking about last night.

He studied her. Had he seen through her, read her thoughts? She thought perhaps he had, and that would never do. She made her way to the front door and he followed. "Thank you again," she said, and she was certain there could be no doubt in his mind she wanted him to leave.

He leaned in to kiss her cheek. Was he really going to continue that facade? She leaned back out of his reach.

He frowned momentarily. "Oh, of course," he said, and touched his nose. "Too many eyes and ears around."

"Goodbye, Jeremy," she said abruptly. Was this the last time she ever saw him? Probably not, but from this moment forward, they were friends and nothing more. All she needed to do now was get that message through to Jeremy.

"I'll do what I always do," Jeremy announced. "I will do my utmost to ensure every adult in Dewberry has a will."

As Ivy glanced around the table she took in the grins. Practically every committee member was either grinning or holding back a grin. She wanted to ask what was so funny, but she already knew. Annie had made the decision for him, and yet again, Jeremy was doing exactly what he had been told to do.

"What about you, Ivy? Have you made a decision yet?" All eyes were suddenly on her, and Ivy wanted to crawl beneath the table. Why did Jeremy have to single her out anyway? No one else on the committee had declared their intentions.

"I, um…" She really hadn't made her decision as yet. "I have a few ideas, but I'm not sure which one I'll go with yet." And she wasn't. They all required far more energy than she had these days. She wasn't ill, she was certain of it. Then again, did a broken heart count?

Jeremy had made things difficult by calling in to the store every chance he had. Bringing sandwiches and cake, and even bottled water. She'd enjoyed their time at the pergola, despite knowing she shouldn't. She wanted to tell him not to call again, but she didn't have the heart. She knew she would miss him deeply, far more than as just a friend.

She missed being held in his arms and being kissed by Jeremy, although it had only been a few days since it happened. Had he realized he'd gone too far if all he wanted was friendship? Perhaps her message had finally gotten through.

"Go on, tell us then."

"Yes, please do."

Mutterings around the table left her little choice. "One idea I had was to show the ladies how to pack their travel bag." This time, there were low mutterings. Disapproval? She wasn't sure. "How to repurpose a hat was another idea. I did think about showing them how to freshen up an old gown, but honestly, I'd be doing myself a disservice." Ivy sat back in her seat and glanced about. No one said a word – were those ideas really so awful?

"I really like your first idea," Holly from the *Holly-Berry Cake Shoppe* said. "A lot of our ladies travel to visit relatives, so it would be quite helpful." She scribbled something on her notebook. "Like Jeremy, I'll probably do what I do every other year – a demonstration of cake decorating. We can't give all our secrets away or we would lose all our customers." She winked at Ivy. "And that would defeat the purpose."

"I'm going to do a demonstration of how I make boiled candy," Belle said.

"I'll probably do the same as last year and read a passage from a recent book." Noelle wrote something on her notepad then suddenly glanced up. "Actually, no. I've changed my mind. I'm going to hold a book club. Everyone will have to buy the book to join in." She clapped her hands together in delight. She took a mouthful of water as though celebrating her decision.

Ivy glanced at Jeremy, who winked at her. Did he still have feelings for her? She'd tried everything to make him understand theirs was a friendship, not a romantic relationship, but he was having none of it.

"Is that it? Are we done?" he said, suddenly jumping up out of his chair as though he'd already made the decision. He glanced across at the fire. Ivy noticed the embers were getting low, so they wouldn't have to wait around too long for it to die down. Besides, Jeremy was likely to throw water on it to quell the fire if need be.

He came across as an impatient man at times, and yet his occupation told her otherwise. As a solicitor, he would surely need patience to deal with some of his more irritating clients, and Ivy had no doubt there were many. Even with her own business, there were customers who could be quite infuriating, but she didn't have the luxury of hurrying them up. She wanted their business and that was not the way to gain customers, but rather to lose them. She sighed as she stood. Was this extravaganza fiasco even worth her time and effort? Ivy was beginning to think not, but she recalled Mrs. Grayson's words and knew Aunt Mildred would have been beyond disappointed if she didn't participate. After all, it was a tradition, or at least that's what Ivy had been told. Whether it was true or not was another thing entirely.

"Ready to leave?" She was startled out of her thoughts when Jeremy touched her shoulder. "Where did you go?" he wanted to know. He studied her then glanced back toward the fire, no doubt checking it was properly out.

"I was thinking about my aunt and how she would want me to participate in this whole…" she waved her hands about "debacle."

He chuckled. "I often wonder about it myself. Do I get more clients because of it? I highly doubt it since I'm the only solicitor in town and there's not another one for at least one hundred miles. But Annie likes arranging it, and she tells me it lifts my profile." He rolled his eyes. "I also question that likelihood."

Ivy moved toward the door and snatched up her coat from the rack. "Here, let me," Jeremy said quietly, then helped Ivy into her warm coat. "I'm certain it will be quite cold outside. We had a light spattering of snow this afternoon. Did you see it at all?"

"I've been far too busy lately. Mrs. Grayson seems to spread word like wildfire." As she put her arms into the coat, their fingers brushed. Ivy shivered. How was she supposed to keep her distance when Jeremy insisted on accompanying her everywhere? He stared down at her. Did he feel it too?

She wouldn't mind so much if their relationship was going somewhere, but when a man declared he had a *fondness* for you, what were you meant to believe? For Ivy, it meant he wanted nothing more than her friendship.

And yet he kissed her.

It was a perplexing situation, and not one Ivy knew how to handle. "That old bird is nothing but a gossip," he snarled, and a dark expression crossed his face. "Shall we go?" His hand to her back, he ushered her down the stairs. "Brace yourself for the cold. Where are your gloves?" he suddenly asked.

"Oh! I must have left them back there." Back in that room. The one she really didn't want to be alone with Jeremy in. Not because she didn't trust him. It was more she didn't trust herself. She liked him far too much.

He unlocked the door to the Executive Suite and led her inside. "There they are," he said. "Right where you were sitting." He hurried over and snatched them up.

She stood with her back to the wall while she waited. "This really is a beautiful room," she said dreamily. "Quite romantic." The moment the words were out of her mouth, she flinched. Why on earth did she say that? It was true – the room did feel rather romantic, but it was a very poor choice of words when she was there alone with Jeremy Hycroft, who liked to kiss women he didn't love.

"It is rather," he said with a grin on his face. He handed her the gloves and she turned to leave. "Ivy," he said breathlessly, and she turned to face him. Before she knew what was happening, she was in his arms. It felt so nice, and she'd missed it. Missed being held like this.

She molded into him, and his arms tightened around her. When she glanced up, he leaned down and kissed her, and she kissed him back. Until she realized exactly what she was doing. "This is nice," she said. "But we shouldn't." She began to pull out of his arms.

He frowned. "You don't like it?"

"That's the problem. I do like it."

"Then what's the problem?" He looked puzzled. Did Jeremy Hycroft see her as a fling of some sort? Because Ivy wasn't that sort of woman. It was all or nothing with her, but apparently Jeremy didn't feel the same.

"I'd like to go home now if you don't mind." She turned and ran down the stairs. By the time Jeremy arrived, she was almost out the door.

"Ivy, wait," he called after her. "Please?" She stopped then but wasn't sure she should have lingered. Perhaps it was better if she ran ahead. But it was dark, and she didn't like walking home alone in the dark, so she did what he asked.

He pulled his collar up around his neck, and Ivy repositioned her scarf. It was quite chilly, far colder than it had been last week when they had the meeting. With Christmas approaching, at least there would be few meetings left.

He locked the door to the town hall then hooked his arm through Ivy's. They were both silent for a few minutes then he turned to face her. "What is all this about? I thought we were getting on well."

"We were," she said then licked her lips. "We still are."

He looked even more confused. "So, what's the problem then?"

Should she tell him or just pretend she'd changed her mind? She took a deep breath and stared up at him. "The problem is," she said quietly, "I don't have a *fondness* for you." She watched as he swallowed. She'd hurt his feelings. "What I mean is…"

He interrupted her. "No, please don't. I understand."

Did he? Did he really understand she'd fallen in love with him but couldn't bear the fact it wasn't reciprocated?

"Here we are," he said, reaching for her key. "I'll see you inside." He took Ivy to her private residence then left, not even attempting to kiss her cheek as he usually did. "I'll lock up as I leave," he said, handing her the keys.

"Thank you," she said in a small voice. Jeremy was a good man, a man she could love with all her heart. Only he didn't love her back, and that just wouldn't do.

Chapter Seven

Jeremy made his way along Dewberry Lane with his hands shoved in his pockets and his shoulders slumped. Ivy's words rolled over and over in his head. He thought they'd become close and believed she felt the same way he did. Thought she loved him.

He'd dated many women over the years, more because they'd near forced themselves on him, rather than him showing any interest. Jeremy had never really been all that interested in women. His business had always come first.

But it was more than that, and he knew it. The truth of the matter was, he had never crossed paths with the right woman. His parents had been forced into a marriage of convenience, and neither had ever really been happy. Father, an up and coming solicitor at the time, had been forced to marry a young woman who ran in high society circles. He was promised it would escalate his career, and it had, but it had caused him nothing but misery.

Jeremy had seen the result of that. Oh, Father had supported his family, and he'd never let them down. Joshua Hycroft had ensured his son had the best education, and made certain he went to the most prestigious law school in the country, to follow in his father's footsteps. Sadly, he'd never been a particularly happy man. His mother was despondent most of the time, and the environment at home had affected Jeremy. For most of his adult life, he'd avoided becoming attached to the opposite sex.

Father had tried to push him into marriage, and had been persistent in his efforts. He had him all but walking down the aisle with Mary Conifer not twelve months before he'd died. But Jeremy resisted, much to Mary's disgust, and here he was now, one of the most sought-after bachelors in Dewberry.

He sighed. It's not like he'd been overly ambitious with Ivy. Had he? Was he being overzealous? He rolled his eyes. He didn't think he had been. No matter now – it was too late. She'd all but told him to leave her alone. The thought of not seeing Ivy ever again shattered his heart into a million pieces.

~*~

Ivy stood behind the counter folding clothes ready to go into boxes. She'd had a lovely burst of sales lately. She was not unhappy about that fact.

This afternoon she had another shipment of garments arriving, and that would keep her more than a little busy. She wrote up the invoice for this particular box of garments then placed it inside. She reached for the ribbon to secure the box but glanced up when the bell over the door jingled.

Jeremy. She wasn't certain she could deal with him today. She'd had a prolonged night of tossing and turning, and barely had any sleep. One thing she'd never done before is harden her heart, but in this case, it's what she needed to do. Entering into a loveless relationship, or even a loveless marriage, was not something she was prepared to do.

"Good morning, Ivy," he said, his voice sounding defeated. She glanced up at him and his expression was bleak. He had the darkest circles under his eyes, and she figured she probably looked equally as bad.

"Jeremy," she said tersely. She was certain she'd made her position clear last night. It might not be what she wanted, but it was required. It was all or nothing. *Love or nothing.* Each time she thought about it, her heart shattered a little more. Soon there would be nothing left to harm.

"I didn't sleep well last night," he said quietly. Was he looking for sympathy, because she was in the exact same boat. "I…I had no idea you hated me so much," he said, glancing toward the floor.

Her head snapped up. Jeremy thought she hated him? He couldn't be further from the truth. "I…"

The bell over the door jingled.

"Damn it," he said under his breath.

Mrs. Jolimont entered the store to collect her purchases, and Ivy handed them over. "Thank you," she said quietly then saw the woman out of the store.

"Honestly, Jeremy," she said when they were alone again, "did I say I hated you?"

He opened his mouth to speak when the bell jingled again. "It is incredibly difficult to talk here," he said, his voice full of frustration. "Can we meet later – for supper perhaps?"

Ivy let out the breath she'd been holding. "I don't think that's a good idea." Mrs. Halliday stepped into the store and Jeremy turned away. "I'll pick you up at six," he said as though she hadn't already refused. He waved with his back to her as he left the store.

"Mr. Hycroft looks awful," the customer said. "Is he ill?"

Ivy stared at her. Was she his keeper? It wasn't as though everyone in Dewberry knew they'd been stepping out together. "I have no idea, Mrs. Halliday."

The woman stared her down, until finally. she let her views be known. "Well," she huffed, "since the man is courting you, it is your business to know." She snatched up her package and stormed out of *Buttons and Bows*.

Is that what everyone in town thought? That she and Jeremy Hycroft were stepping out together? She put her hands to her face. It was far worse than she'd imagined. She'd been blissfully unaware what people were saying about them, but now it had come to bite them. Quite badly perhaps.

She finished packing her orders and put them aside, and once more the bell jingled. She did like the store being busy, but it seemed she didn't get a moment to herself anymore. She hadn't so much as tidied even one display today, and it was an ongoing task.

She glanced up to find her delivery had arrived. Was it really that late? The clock confirmed it was already afternoon. Several boxes were stacked outside the store, and she rushed over to hold the door open for the man delivering her order. It was far more convenient to have someone deliver them from the train station than for her to have to do it herself. She was certain her aunt would have done the exact same thing. In fact, she seemed to recall that being the case on one of her visits some years ago.

She glanced down the shopping strip to see Jeremy sitting on one of the wooden benches there. It was snowing lightly, and he was being covered in snow. She itched to go to him but couldn't. Ivy had to hold the door open for the boxes to be carried inside. The moment they were all inside, she paid for the delivery then rushed outside to Jeremy.

"What are you doing?" she demanded.

He glanced up at her as though he hadn't seen her there. "I can't stop thinking about…what happened." Ivy couldn't help but feel sorry for him since she felt the same way.

"Did you know everyone in Dewberry thinks you are courting me?" she again demanded, beginning to feel the cold.

For the first time today, he grinned. "Of course," he said, then his grin faded, because now they weren't. "We really need to talk," he said, his mood dark again.

"I can't do it now," Ivy said quietly. "I have customers collecting orders most of the day, and I have ten boxes waiting for me to open them and put the garments away."

He nodded. "I understand," he said then stood, brushing the snow from his thick coat. "Where is your coat?" he demanded, suddenly noticing she wasn't wearing one and was shivering.

"It's upstairs. I didn't have time to grab it." She turned and began walking back to the store.

Jeremy reached out and grabbed her hand. "Don't leave me," he pleaded then pulled her close, enveloping her in his arms and his warmth. He leaned down and covered her mouth. She resisted for a moment then relaxed. This was exactly what she wanted, but didn't at the same time.

She pulled back and looked up at him. "I can't do this now," she said breathlessly. "Besides, everyone can see us."

He laughed. "Honestly, I don't care who sees us," he said then let go of her hands. He pulled out his pocket watch. "I have to go anyway. I have a client coming shortly."

"I have to leave too," she said then turned and hastily made her way back to *Buttons and Bows*.

What a dilemma she found herself in. Perhaps when they talked it out tonight, they would agree to go their separate ways. No matter how she looked at it, Ivy knew she would miss Jeremy with all her heart.

As promised, Jeremy picked her up at six. They slowly walked to Ma's Kitchen. Was Jeremy hoping she would open up to him on the way there? A man could hope, couldn't he? But it wasn't to be. Ivy didn't say a word.

He loved the feel of her on his arm. He was proud to have her beside him. She was a beautiful woman after all, and genteel, unlike some of the women he had dated. One such woman he couldn't get out of his mind was Jolene Harrigan. She was a fireball if ever there was one. Jolene was so determined to marry him; she'd even tried to entice him into bed with her.

Like every other hot-blooded man, he'd considered the offer, but decided against it. Apart from the fact it went against everything he believed in, Jeremy was certain all she wanted was to force him to marry her. And she would get the best side of that deal, there was no doubt about it. He almost shivered at the thought of it – he'd certainly dodged a bullet with that one.

He'd heard Jolene married Alex Drimane six months later. He was one of the most prosperous ranchers around these parts. Jeremy truly hoped they were both happy.

"Are you all right, Jeremy?" Ivy's voice brought him out of his thoughts, which probably wasn't a bad thing. He was normally quite chatty, especially with Ivy, but tonight he was more thoughtful. At the top of his reflections was how tonight would go.

"Hmmm? Yes, I'm fine. I have a few things on my mind." As he was sure Ivy did too. Tonight could change their entire lives, no matter which way things went. "I asked Merry to give us one of the booths up the back of the diner. It is quieter and far more private there." They would need privacy. He didn't want the entire town knowing their business, although, it seemed like they already did. It was typical of Dewberry. But despite the fact there was little privacy, he loved this place, loved living here.

She swallowed hard then nodded. They both knew why they were here, so he wasn't sure why she looked so anxious. Although, if he was truthful with himself, Jeremy was somewhat nervous too. He'd become far too fond of Ivy to lose her now, and it seemed he was already on the brink of that happening.

Once inside the little diner, Merry saw them seated in the booth. The place was almost empty, which was often the case mid-week. With the fire roaring not far away from their booth, the place was pleasantly warm. A lovely change from the icy weather they'd endured on their way here.

After placing their orders, Merry left them alone. Jeremy didn't want to talk about their situation yet – all that would achieve was to spoil their appetites. He leaned over and covered Ivy's hand. It felt good, and he never wanted to let it go. Ivy, on the other hand, looked a little uncomfortable, and even wriggled in her seat at one point. But then she smiled.

"Have you finalized your extravaganza plans yet," Jeremy asked, keeping away from the main topic of discussion.

"I have," she said, a smile still on her face. "I've decided to do the travel thing."

"What is that exactly," Jeremy asked. "I don't understand it."

She chuckled. Had he said something funny? He hadn't thought so. "It's a special way to fold your clothes so they resist wrinkling while traveling."

"Oh," he said as though he understood, but in reality, didn't. He had no intention of showing himself to be a fool when it came to issues about women so said nothing further.

"And you? Have you decided?"

Of course he had. At least Annie had. "I will be discussing the exciting topic of wills and why everyone should have one." He squeezed her hand and grinned. He didn't really mind talking about wills, but it got rather tedious year after year. If only there was a way to spruce the subject up. He'd had plenty of practice now, and surely if there was a way, he'd have thought of it by now.

Merry placed their food in front of them, and they linked hands for the blessing. "Thank you, Lord, for this food, and for the special friendship between us. Amen." When he opened his eyes and glanced up, Ivy was looking at him strangely. Had he gone too far? He didn't think so. "Tuck in while it's hot," he said.

Each time he glanced across at Ivy as they ate, she dipped her head. It was as though she was afraid to look at him. Or perhaps, she simply didn't want to see him. Could it be he was right, that she hated him? If that were the case, why did she agree to come to supper with him tonight? Or was it because he'd insisted?

When their soiled plates were removed, Ivy began to speak, but their desserts were delivered to them almost immediately. "Eat first, remember," he said when Merry was out of earshot. He didn't want to be turned off his food, and Jeremy knew that's what would happen if they discussed their situation now. Normally, he enjoyed company at supper, especially when that company was Ivy, but tonight was different.

Tonight, his stomach was tied in knots, and it was doing somersaults, making him feel poorly. But he pushed on. They needed to resolve their differences once and for all. Merry returned with mugs of coffee and glanced at him with a puzzled look on her face. Likely because every other time he'd come here with Ivy they'd both been gloriously happy. Tonight, they were both subdued.

He said not a word, and Merry disappeared back into the kitchen.

Ivy ate the last mouthful of her apple crumble, and Jeremy gulped down a mouthful of coffee having already finished his dessert. It was time. Who would speak first, he wondered.

"Let me get one thing straight," Ivy said forcefully. He had to force back a smile. She would always have the first say if the opportunity arose. "I do not hate you."

Her words shocked him, although, if he was truthful, they shouldn't have. She let him hold her and kiss her earlier today. "I'm very pleased to hear it," he said quietly then took another sip of coffee. If he kept quiet, would she open herself up to him? Tell him how she really felt? It was one of the techniques he used as a solicitor, and it usually worked.

"It's quite the opposite, to be honest." She leaned back in her chair with her arms crossed. He raised his eyebrows but still refrained from speaking. "The problem is…" She breathed deeply, and at one point, Jeremy thought she might hyperventilate. She swallowed hard. "The problem is you have already declared your *fondness* for me."

That was a problem? He felt the color drain out of his face. How was that a problem? Surely it was a good thing? Perhaps now he should speak. Yet he still delayed the inevitable.

"Do you have nothing to say, Jeremy?"

Ivy looked as though she was about to bolt, and that was the last thing he wanted to happen. He reached for her hand to stop her departure. He'd pondered the question for too long apparently. "I am fond of you, Ivy," he said quietly. "I'm not sure how that has caused this rift between us." She still seemed ready to abscond, but there was little he could do about it.

"Because," she said quietly, her eyes filling with tears, "because *I love you*," she said, tears now rolling down her cheeks.

This was a revelation he hadn't anticipated. His heart thudded, and he was breathless. Ivy loved him? He loved Ivy. Where was the problem?

"I love you too," he said, gently, then pulled her from the booth to kiss her. This time, Ivy didn't object.

Chapter Eight

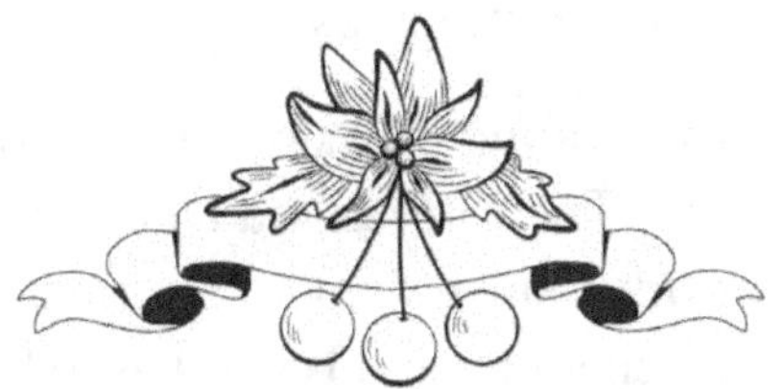

The town was abuzz with the news. Ivy Henderson was engaged to Jeremy Hycroft.

What a revelation, only it really wasn't. The whole town of Dewberry had known for weeks the two were sweet on each other. They'd had a rocky start, there was no doubt, but when they'd finally opened up to each other, the inevitable happened.

And when they took Mrs. Grayson out of the equation, things were far better. "I told you she is an old gossip," Jeremy had told her. He wasn't pleased when he found out the woman had said she would be nothing but a receptible for his heirs. "I'd like to ring her neck," he said, half joking.

They stood side by side outside the town hall where the enormous Christmas tree was being raised. The entire town had come out for the event. A large box had been placed nearby for donations of toys and other items for the less privileged. Mrs. Grayson had left a sizeable number of items and promised to bring more in the coming days.

Christmas was around the corner and excitement filled the air. The stores had all begun their Christmas Extravaganza demonstrations. Each store had their own schedule, and Ivy's was to begin soon. She was even looking forward to it.

Jeremy snaked an arm around her waist. "Your idea was terrific," he said. "We've never done such a thing in Dewberry Lane before." He leaned down and kissed her cheek. "My brilliant fiancée," he said proudly.

Ivy wondered if Aunt Mildred was looking down, watching over them. Jeremy assured her she would be. As the ropes we're pulled by the younger men in town then secured to keep the tree safe, everyone clapped. Even without decorations, it was a sight to behold.

The children all rushed forward with their hand-made decorations and added them to the tree. "This could become a new tradition," Jeremy said quietly. "It even makes the thought of discussing wills seem appealing for once. The excitement of it all, I mean," he continued. "Maybe you can think up some new ideas for next year."

Ivy rolled her eyes. Her future husband was destined to be stuck with wills for the foreseeable future. "I must leave," she said in a rush. "I can see a group of ladies waiting at the store." Jeremy leaned down and kissed her gently, not worrying what anyone thought now they were engaged.

Not in her wildest dreams did Ivy think she would be engaged to be married before Christmas. They hadn't set a date yet, but Jeremy promised it wouldn't be long. He was anxious to make her his wife.

As Ivy hurried toward the store, she could feel his eyes burning into her back. "Good afternoon, ladies," she said, helping them out of their coats. She already had chairs set up and ready for each person who had booked in for the demonstration. As each woman took her seat, Ivy glanced around. It wasn't so long ago most of these women were strangers to her. Today, they were her friends and customers.

She waited until everyone sat comfortably before beginning. She held up a shirt then laid it down on the low table she'd added so everyone could comfortably watch. "Our demonstration today is designed to teach you how to pack your clothes so they won't wrinkle as badly when you travel."

As she began to fold the arms in then roll the garment, the room was filled with oohs and aahs. She glanced up to see grins all round. "Who would like to try," she asked, and everyone jumped up from their seats.

"Did those new nightgowns arrive," Mrs. Jensen asked.

Not to be outdone, Mrs. Carson asked about the latest style gown.

Soon, the store was abuzz with ladies participating in her demonstration, as well as making purchases. It was a good day all round.

Everything happened at once.

One minute, Ivy was contemplating setting up garment racks, and the next, she was preparing to be married. Jeremy had suddenly decided four days before Christmas he could wait no more. He booked the preacher then told Ivy.

She was aghast. "But I don't have a wedding gown," she said, horrified at this sudden change of events.

"You have a store full of them," he said as he grinned.

"I don't have wedding shoes," she told him.

He reached out and held her hands. "I'm not going to look at your feet."

No matter what she said, he had an answer. "What about…"

"Whatever the problem, I'll find a solution," he said gently, putting his fingers to her lips. "Do you love me?" He looked at her curiously.

"You know I do."

"Then forget everything else. It will be a small affair since it is so rushed. I hope you don't mind?"

Mind? She felt relieved. Ivy knew if they waited too long, the entire town of Dewberry would get in on the act. Especially Mrs. Grayson, who seemed to want to take Ivy under her wing. No doubt because of her friendship with Aunt Mildred. She really was a dear lady – she just needed to stop interfering. It almost broke her and Jeremy apart.

As she stood at the back of the church, Ivy breathed deeply. Was she really doing this? It seemed so sudden. But apart from her original objections about not having a proper wedding gown and shoes, everything was perfect.

The atmosphere was electric. Everyone in town was excited – and were all packed into the little church.

There hadn't been a wedding for some years, they'd told Ivy, which made it even more exciting. As the organ music began to play, Mrs. Grayson leaned in to whisper in her ear. "Are you ready, my dear?" Ivy nodded. "Our dear Mildred would have been so proud," she said as she swiped at an errant tear. "And so very happy for you and Jeremy." She pulled a handkerchief from her reticule and blotted her tears.

"I believe they're waiting for us," Ivy pointed out, and they began to walk slowly down the aisle. Jeremy stood at the front, wearing his best suit, and turned to study her. The grin on his face filled her with warmth.

And to think, without Aunt Mildred's death, they may never have met. A tear trickled down her face at the thought. "Having second thoughts," he asked, a frown now on his face.

She shook her head. "Thinking about my aunt."

He reached out and wiped her tears away. "Mildred would have approved," he said quietly. "I know she would have."

The preacher cleared his throat. "Are you ready," he asked, and proceeded when they both agreed. "Dearly Beloved…"

Soon, the ceremony was over and they were married. "You may kiss your bride," the preacher announced, and that's exactly what Jeremy did. Then he swooped her up and almost ran out of the church.

The townspeople followed them out and threw rice at them, then they all headed toward Ma's Kitchen, where Jeremy had arranged an informal wedding breakfast.

Ivy sat back in their private booth where they'd sorted out their issues not so long ago. This was going to be her most memorable Christmas ever.

Epilogue

One year later…

The raising of the Christmas tree was about to begin. The people of Dewberry decided it was a nice tradition, something that brought everyone together.

The donation box had worked well last year, and they were able to distribute toys and food to all those in need. Mrs. Grayson was the biggest donor; Ivy had harbored no doubts that would be the case.

"My dear girl," Mrs. Grayson said, exasperated, "should you even be here?" She looked mortified.

"Get your wife a chair immediately, Mr. Hycroft," she demanded, but Ivy simply laughed.

"I am perfectly fine," she told the older woman. "I have my last demonstration at the store shortly, then I shall close up for the day.

Mrs. Grayson huffed. "I should think so! A woman in your condition shouldn't be seen, let alone running demonstrations in your store." Ivy glanced up at Jeremy. She could barely stop herself from laughing, and it appeared, neither could he.

As she wandered away from them, Jeremy leaned down and whispered. "What do you think? Shall I get you a chair?"

Ivy glared at him. When did he start listening to what Mrs. Grayson said anyway? "I do not need a chair," she said through gritted teeth. "Oh!" She suddenly let out a small shriek.

Jeremy stared down at her. "Ivy?"

She waved her hands about then glanced up at him. "I'm fine. It's only the baby moving a little more vigorously than usual."

He frowned. "Are you sure? I can get the doc…"

"I'm sure." She crossed her arms, and he knew she was serious. The moment the tree was raised and secured, she headed toward *Buttons and Bows*. She had grown very fond of the store, and despite Jeremy wanting her to hire staff to allow her to stay home, she would have none of it. It was her store after all. Besides, she loved the place.

As she continued to walk, her baby continued to protest, until it got to a point she could walk no further. She leaned against the wall of one of the stores and held her stomach. "No, baby," she whispered. "It's too early." If you called two days too early, that was. Jeremy was by her side and lifted her into his arms before she slid to the ground. He would be rather put out if she told him she'd been having contractions since the early hours of the morning. She was determined to get this last demonstration over with before her baby arrived.

"I'm sorry, ladies, but the demonstration is cancelled," Jeremy said as he carried her past the store.

Mrs. Grayson came scurrying toward them. "I told you to get her a chair," she said firmly, trailing after Jeremy. "I'll run ahead and warn the doctor." And that's exactly what she did.

Jeremy paced up and down the path outside the doctor's office. He had done so for some hours now. Far too many thoughts went through his mind. The one that bothered him the most – would Ivy survive this ordeal?

Doctor Matthew Wigham was a middle-aged man who had been practicing in Dewberry for some years now, and was highly regarded. Jeremy was sure he could trust the doctor, and Mrs. Grayson had reassured him. He had delivered many babies in Dewberry, she'd said, and would ensure Ivy came through her ordeal safely.

Still, it didn't provide the assurance Jeremy needed. He knew anything could happen. He'd listened to his wife's screams all afternoon, and at one point, Mrs. Grayson directed him away from the doctor's rooms, taking him to Ma's Kitchen.

She filled him with coffee until he could take no more. Then he returned to where he'd been before and paced once more. Until finally, the doctor's nurse fetched him – the baby had arrived.

He was more than a little agitated by the time he was by his wife's side. He stared down at Ivy; their baby cradled in her arms. A tear trickled down his face, and he wiped it away.

"Meet your son," Ivy said wearily. She looked exhausted. "I thought we could call him Joshua Roderick. Would you like to hold him?"

The doctor nodded at him to take the baby. "Your wife is exhausted and needs to rest," he said. "Take the baby, at least for now."

He did as instructed. "I understand Joshua, after my father," Jeremy said gently. "But not Roderick."

"After my father," she told him as her eyes began to flutter closed. Jeremy looked down into his newborn son's face. "Joshua Roderick," he said gently as a shiver went through him. "Thank you, Lord," he said quietly. "For blessing me with a wonderful family."

Jeremy held the baby close to his heart, which was full to the brim with love.

The End

From the Author

Thank you so much for reading my book – I hope you enjoyed it.

I would greatly appreciate you leaving a review where you purchased, even if it is only a one-liner. It helps to have my books more visible!

About the Author

Multi-published, award-winning and bestselling author, Cheryl Wright, former secretary, debt collector, account manager, writing coach, and shopping tour hostess, loves reading.

She writes both historical and contemporary western romance, as well as romantic suspense.

She lives in Melbourne, Australia, and is married with two adult children and has six grandchildren. When she's not writing, she can be found in her craft room making greeting cards.

Links:

Website: *http://www.cheryl-wright.com/*

Blog: *http://romance-authors.com/*

Facebook Reader Group:
https://www.facebook.com/groups/cherylwrightauthor/

Join My Newsletter:

https://cheryl-wright.com/newsletter/

www.ingramcontent.com/pod-product-compliance
Lightning Source LLC
Chambersburg PA
CBHW070631120726
47909CB00004B/1389